John Collins

Two Essays on Constitutional Reform

SALZWASSER
VERLAG

John Collins

Two Essays on Constitutional Reform

Reprint of the original, first published in 1859.

1st Edition 2023 | ISBN: 978-3-37513-838-7

Verlag (Publisher): Salzwasser Verlag GmbH, Zeilweg 44, 60439 Frankfurt, Deutschland
Vertretungsberechtigt (Authorized to represent): E. Roepke, Zeilweg 44, 60439 Frankfurt, Deutschland
Druck (Print): Books on Demand GmbH, In de Tarpen 42, 22848 Norderstedt, Deutschland

TWO ESSAYS

ON

CONSTITUTIONAL REFORM.

TWO ESSAYS

ON

ONSTITUTIONAL REFORM.

BY

JOHN COLLINS,

AUTHOR OF "THE FALL OF MAN."

I.—THE ASPECT OF SOCIETY.
II.—OFFICE, AND THE COMPETITIVE SYSTEM.

LONDON:

IGMAN, BROWN, GREEN, LONGMANS, AND ROBERTS.

DUBLIN: W. CURRY & CO. EDINBURGH: A. & C. BLACK.

1859.

PREFACE.

The object of the writer, in these Essays, is to direct public attention to some aspects of Constitutional Reform,
which he believes have been rather overlooked, than de-
preciatingly viewed, in a too isolating consideration of
Reform, as depending on the much inferior agitation
and topic of the Franchise.

The present aspect of the Constitution is of the gravest
moment; and the melioration likewise, in their working,
of the several agencies for the expression of the voice and
power of Opinion—both those which are *active*, and which
are *slumbering*. Literary enterprise, the voices of the
Church, the Press, and public Agitator, and the organs
of Academical Institution,—especially, too, the voices of
the moral members of a Community, expressed in their
individual *acts*, the most neglected, and most potent organ of national opinion. The writer has drawn a special attention, in treating it, to the industrial advance
and elevation of the sex of Woman.

The topic of the second Essay is of an import far more

deep, in national concern, than any question of the Franchise; and it needs no introduction to the Essay. They are offered to the public, for their earnest consideration, supplementary to the agitation of an isolated reform.

It has been the writer's duty, in these Essays, to animadvert upon the party-government of Statesmen. Let it not be thought that he ascribes a want of personal worth, because they *are* such, to any Statesmen. Far from it. He has had the opportunity to have seen enough of these, to know how very much the blame of party-government abuse belongs to their dependents and supporters. Public men are better men—far better men than to the public, through the damaging medium of their party-politics, they look. And there is far less of essential difference between them, than, through the damaging medium of distorted party-politics, there seems. It is the *system* that is wrong—essentially wrong and rotten—and defiles the reputation of the very best of men, who enter on the crooked, doubling pathways of it. The pretentious man may simulate a virtue in it; but the Statesman, who is truly honest, will not affect to represent it, but as a system of defilement. To the moral clean, it is unclean, and, truly, like the entrance on a filthy gutter. He may be clean, so far as frailty is clean —he may be elegantly dressed; but if he goes once into it, infallibly he will be dirtied. " Ay," said an eminent public friend to this, once speaking to the writer, "and " the cleaner he is by nature, the dirtier he will look after " it."

The truth is, that public men, from the debasing contact of the system, are only to be rightly represented charitably. As public men, they must be viewed to be curtailed of much of their inherited endowment of the good —they must be viewed, emphatically to speak, as " under " nature, and not so good as themselves." Still, alas! there will be meditation for the moralist upon the best of them. The very best are tainted; and, after all the moral eminence of life, there seems too oft (pertaining fallen to the best) some architectural flaw, some cracked entablature—some gap, some leaky vent, some *residue* of the rogue of old mortality.

Of the Literary, and his brother workmen, the writer could not be thought that he indulged uncharitably. Yet he has been constrained to bring a heavy allegation of their public dereliction. The opening Essay will show the several paths wherein, he thinks, that duty to the public is neglected by the Literary. It will show, he humbly hopes also, the high import of the intimations of the times, that *now* is the time for the literateur to assume his right pre-eminence as a guider of the People. It is discreditable to the literary men of our time, that they should hide in nooks and corners, instead of boldly coming out, like their political brothers, utilitarian on the platform of the world. The literateur must come out and be, like all men, practical. If he does not, others will take, as they habitually take, *his* rightful place, who are not qualified (as he is qualified) to benefit his working brothers of Mankind.

No man, or no class of men, can benefit others, without first benefiting themselves. Their status and position, to confer a benefit on others, must of necessity do a benefit to themselves. Heretofore, the literary men have trusted to political, and to everybody, to protect their interests; and *everybody* has protected, very properly—not the literary interests—but the interests pre-eminently of themselves. The literateur has been left to the consolation of knowing that his labours benefit Mankind, and are freely used as a commodity by every class-folk of the world, but himself; and he himself is charitably given, by the knowing ones, his own beef-bone to pick!

He has not even an organization to exhibit himself. This is what all other class-folk of the world studiously endeavour for their interests to unite, and what the literateur pre-eminently wants. Alas! that there is no " local ha-"bitation" for the work of thought in its beginning—no *where*, for the literary commodity to be genuine exhibited. Every commodity has its place to be exhibited; but the loftiest aspiration, and its hierophant, are denied what is enjoyed in liberty by the humblest vendor of a cabbage! The literateur must *talk*, not only *write* his writing. He must talk *lowly* to the low, and *act* utilitarian. It is the duty of the eminent amongst the literary, to change this downward state of things. They can do it only by their high example, standing out to benefit others. They must stand out unselfishly to benefit others. Let them never doubt, that organization soon will gather round

. them, the moment they are felt as public men to be utilitarian, as well as high aspiring. It is a mistake, to
think the two are ever set in contradiction—are ever,
in their practical and forming elements, opposed and
contradicting. They harmonize much rather. The
Mind becomes too abstract, when given isolating to
subjective things. The world's path can only furnish
concrete elements. And greatly would the aspect of
Literature itself be improved, by the mingling of its
workmen in the practical paths of utility.

Earnestly then, and from the motive of a double duty,
would the writer call the literary attention to the observations in his opening Essay. Sure he is, that the Literary have deeply neglected that duty, as a duty which
is owing to their own interests and to themselves. It is
his earnest hope, that many of them may be yet led into
a more right apprehension of the path of duty, that will
be profitable to the Public, as well as to the literary interests and to themselves. It is his earnest hope, that
they will be led into that path of duty—if not for the
literary interests—at least for the interests of their common brothers of the People. He has made his humble
effort, in the hope that others, who are more prominent
and able, may " do likewise."

J. C.

9, CORNISH-TERRACE, RATHMINES,
DUBLIN, *October* 4, 1859.

THE ASPECT OF SOCIETY.

FEW persons, who reflect at all, can have failed to observe one thing in the changing phases of the world's political fashion:—and that is, the growing intensity with which the consideration of moral questions, that are allied to politic, is viewed by all classes of the public *outside* the legislative and representative bodies; and the growing intimations of felt incapacity, on the part of the members of these bodies, to deal with questions of the sort—an incapacity which does not belong to these individuals as *members* of the general public, but as *representative* members of the public. Hence, the Legislator has become, in self-defence, the moral agitator; and he has trenched upon the ground and the domain (all practically abandoned by its own professors) of the Church, the organs of Academical Institution, and of Literature.

It is profitable to examine into the causes of these things:—for it will be seen that we are, none of us, enough aware, that a mighty change has come over the spirit of our Constitution; and a duty has fallen upon thoughtful men to register their honest experiences,

away from political bias or its action, if the enduring interests of the world may be furthered by it.

It is plain, that we are not as we were—that the
mighty revolution which the publicity of Parliamentary
debate, and a free Press through the country, have produced, has in reality transferred the supreme power of the
Commons of the Realm outwards to the people. The
voice of the people no longer speaks through its representatives. They speak now, and are obeyed, as mouth-
piece rather, *by* their representatives—*the public voice is
representative of itself.*

This is a pregnant fact—mighty in its pregnancy—
since the womb of the Revolution brought forth the
startling fact, whose fulness we must recognise,—that
the House of Commons now has eaten out all other
powers, and represents all power in the State.

It is a grave and solemn thing, to think upon such
high responsibility. Who exercises it? Alas! we truly
know it not. The people's representatives do not. The
influencing Statesman with his patronage, the Press, the
public Agitator, all organs of Opinion—these are several
working, and they work their medley in the State.

What is the influence of the Statesman? Let any
public statesman answer—is honesty in *it?* Party there
has done its evil work ; and when the great confederation
of party is corrupt, the patriot must sink. Is not confederate party all corrupt ?—a league of rottenness, to
displace the honest striving of parental, fruitful emulation.

What a glory is in the freedom of emulation. It inspirits man, when prizes are before him—when he can see his way to a possession, can bear it off, and feel that he is worthy. That feeling elevates him, a citizen and a man. He goes abroad, benignant lightened. His visage and his aims are prompted to things honest; for the kindling feeling is before him, that the world was honest to him. How different in the man, the irritated feeling to be supplanted. Moroseness gendered in a heart of worth—a worthless head, a worthless heart, uplifted and promoted.

Is this not, truly, how the party spirit works? " Claims " upon a party," are made the substitute for " qualified " fitness;" and thus, the double wrong—unto the public, and to the qualified man. What sinks of foul iniquity are the party-governing Statesman's channelled courses— struggling in the fight of weary contradiction, to do an honest duty, and to make supporting rottenness cohere.

What elevating influence upon the people's voice can He exert? Does he not depress it rather, till the very agency, that ought to invigorate, is directed to corrupt —till the governing Statesman is held out to be the public fountain to send waters of corruption through the land, to stay its enterprise, and blight the wholesome spirit of its emulation.

Thanks to even corruption—corruption forces on purgation; and public competition for the office of the State is yet the thing, but dawning now in its beginning, which yet will pull down all the power of the party Statesman, and leave opinion, and the power of opinion, free at least from one thing—the Ruler's power to buy and trade upon it, to the perilling of the true advance of power that is wed to enterprise, to moral culture, and to elevation in the State.

The Press again—how influences It the voice of power in the People ?   Like a great Estate of the Realm, centering all the written words of spoke debate, and comment on them—centering the record of the public million acts, and comment on them.   Is *it* a healthy influence, or is it an organ of corruption ?

Of all, it is the healthiest influence, though it is preeminently an organ of corruption.   The party-governing Statesman's blight is on it; and, so long as the agents of the free press are manacled by ties of interest to party—so long as the power of the party-governing Statesman may buy with patronage its service, that service will be menial service and a prostituted service. It will not be the service of the pure and elevated, of the . higher cultured and the moral cultured, of the men who honest work, and who are paid for honest work from the proper and legitimate sources of a revenue.

Of all the agencies which sway the power of the people, the Press has the pre-eminence.   It is rather the associated and peculiar expression of the voice and power of the people—tempering by its discord, and moulding by its harmony, the bursting lights of ever fresh intelligence.   Its mission is a great and glorious mission.   It has pulled down in these Realms tyrannies, and all that domineered against the liberty of Man. Controlling the Executive, it has subjugated all the Legislative Estates. It is sending to the populated corners of the Earth the tidings of the growth, and thoughts, and acts of Man. It is feeding all the streamlets from the greater River, which is flowing up and ever on. It has done this, and all of this, though it is stirring with corruption, —though it is harbouring the envious and the low illiterate,—the hooded miscreant,—the placeman ready to be bought,—the cool assassin of all reputation,—and the men of might, and honour, and intellect, and reputation. It is the world's type and effigy; and will ever fly, the impress of the world, a banner to the Nations.

The public Agitator—how moves He the people's power, in the breath of popular opinion? Like a stirring tempest rousing dead-like leaves to instigated action. The giant trunk of a great Nation quivers to the touch. Deep instincts are in the people; and they grow, or are displaced, by knowledge. Sciolism is the weed that grows with knowledge. It more allures, is fastened on as something that is *practical;* and thus false agitation is the ready handmaid, to subvert stability in things.

There never was a time when Instincts are displaced, but followed it a stepping-down from rock to pebbly stone. Foundations, true or false, are rent; and giant is the rent, when sand takes place of rock of stone. We are losing many of our instincts—instincts that refreshed,

and gave a daily life to our conventional action.   Such
is the instinct for a Moral in the Nation.   Convention-
ality has eat it out, till we have thought it trivial, as a
State, to be professors of Religion.   And thus, all questions of the spiritual kind—of such a kind, that moral
spirit might rejoice to feel that they did interest, are
out of date, old-fashioned for the hearing of this lofty
State.

Such is the action, when perverted, of the public Agitator.   Our people are not *educated* for the largeness of
their power.   Our representatives, how many are of the
number of the public Agitator.   The casual one of
liberal enlargement, but conservative of knowledge and
of truth, is drowned in the gregarious crowd—his wise,
benignant influence lost.   No consistent scheme of
high political action is now possible ; but everything is
breathed over by a littleness, which is borrowed from
the fluctuating voices of the people.

Alas ! that we are such, and that we *are* such.   Our
constitutional advance has been, in its effect, to make us
retrograde—to give the power of the Commons from the
representatives to the people ; thus leaving representatives, while yet depriving them of all real power to act
upon their high responsibilities.

And have we retrograded ?—our retrogradation shall
be advance, when we have *educated* the people,   The
real political remedy is then, to elevate the people.   This
must be done—not by the *legislators*, but by the *thinkers*
of the people.   The corrupting power of the legislator

must be diminished, to admit of the moral elevation of the people. And this implies, and this demands, the abolition of the all-demoralizing system of the public patronage.

This is the morbid sore in our anatomy. In my Essay upon Office, I have dwelt upon the real aspect of our political misery. And, so long as the rotten bone of Patronage is left to fester, a plague-spot in the Constitution, so long will *genuine* enterprise be kept out. When the whole Office of the State is thrown open as profession, we may expect, unbiassed by self-interest, to have worthy Statesmen; and, in place of the corrupted political partisan, to have worthy Supporters of them.

But the battle must be fought, I have said, *outside* the Senate, and not *in* it. It must be fought, too, by the lion hand of *literary work*—by a moral Press, under the control of those who are not bought up by the leaders of political sections. It is vain for literary men to say they cannot do it, and to clamour at their wrongs— *they must help themselves.* They must organize. Instead of separating, they must gather round the academic seats of Learning. They must drive the schoolmaster-classes from the now exclusive, and usurped supremacy of them. They must make the Universities by a potency be heard, both in the rightful graduation of all public candidates for Office, and in the criticizing of them in their after public work. They must do it by their able conduct of an independent academic press.

I have lived much in the borders of the world; and I

have seen that all men who would live, must do something to the world's *active* living. Literary men might
command an eminence, if they would only step by the
path of high *utility* to it. They might unite the powers
of the Educational Academies, of the Church, of the
public offices of the State, and all Professions, if they
only *concentrated* their elevated powers thus, to bear
upon the moral moving of the masses.

These are the agencies to substitute for the breath of
the agitator and the demagogue, conservative organs of
Opinion. These are the agencies, worked honest and
worked high, wherewith to meliorate the working Constitution. Genius and the literary enterprise—are not
the thinkers of the world rightly called "the unacknow-
"ledged legislators of Mankind?" And must they ever
be, as they have been, the fruitfullest of active *thought*,
the barrenest of *sense?* What does subsist, utilitarian
in its life, without an organization? Has Genius, Literature, any organization? Are not its treasures used
for a commodity by all but its own makers—its hiero-
phants, the vagabonds of the Earth? Let it erect—and
let the buried bones of its mortality be clothed with
nether life, with strivings to be useful, with genius to
the work.

What are the Educational Academies, the organiza-
tions of University, but fitted for them to engraft in?
In such an Age, the very elements of the Constitution
shifting upon sand, should the prime fountains of the

inspiration and the vigorous thought hold back, and millions stunting? Are scientific men, and the traditionary teachers of a literature, all that the people want, to guide them into light, to wield the absolutism of their constitutional power? They want the comprehensiveness of pure direction. They want the lightening vivid of a bolder instinct—instinct that can group the many things, and put the many things with certain ken to comprehension. They want what mere acquirement cannot impart—they want what *genius*, and no talent, can impart.

Literary men might unite, if they were organized, the powers of the Church. What does the power of the Church now want, to be constraining for the social good, but that—to be united? It is a rented, vast economy —a thing that speaks within the world, without a house —ten thousand living stones, without a hand to gather, and to make them great and glorious edifice.

What is this Church, our National Church? is it alone the Church of the Establishment? It is not only such. All the great conspiring Sects who call on Jesus, and who spread the volume of his heavenly record, are of the true Church in the Nation. They have a right to participate in the preferments of the Nation—their eminent men, to be accounted chief worthy of the extra-clerico preferments of the Nation.

Myself, a member of the Establishment, I cannot speak too much, too sympathizing of them. Men of the most eminent endowments and large acquirement, and whose labours hourly enrich the fruitful field of God's husbandry. Men whose abilities would have led them on to sure preferment in their vocations, if they had been able conscientiously to belong to the Church of the Establishment. And then, to see them faithfully pursuing their Great Master's service, unrequited in the world—depending for the temporal wants of life on humble pastorships, small literary appointment which they may sometimes providentially chance upon, and the scanty auxiliary aid (for their endowment) of underpaid writing for the literary and periodical press.

Nothing ever lost by its enlargement—no more does human thought or interest by its. We are not narrowed, when we co-operate. We may be charitable, and not false. Be honest *for thyself*; and, by no bigot's breath, try thou to damn the right convictions of all others *for themselves*. Cloak not *thy own*, thy truest utterings; or ever seek to wrong the honest breath of *any man*. I have a deep conviction, that every man is bound to have religious and political faith. I have as deep a conviction, that the diversities of Man's types are unutterable, inexplicable as his differences. Concentrate powers abide, and but abide, in Him the Holy One—a fragment part is *every* nature. The man who thinks it, dogmatizes not. He looks, and looks, and lowly looks. It is the greatness of the wise man's wisdom. It is his rank—the joyance of a dignity of nature.

I have been abused, I said, once writing to a dear and

eminent non-conformist friend, for these sentiments. Nevertheless, I am not the less a lover of Catholic truth; and do believe, that the great God of Heaven, whatever of Great and Good inscrutable He may be, is not cast in the type of our narrow conventionalities. I can feelingly sympathize in all your aspirations to adore Him, as your nature (guided by him) prompts you. I can well understand that others know him differently, and from each other differently. There is more harmony in *loving*, than in *thinking*—and may we all, adoring, love him.

This is, no other is, the spirit of a National Church; and, in this spirit only, can the great confederate of Nations render their triumphant harmony of adoration to the King that sitteth on the throne. But the spirit of exclusion is now working, and the bigot heart is never bursting, and the generous life that throes in human breasts dies out in theologic dogmas. Theology is groaning with its dogmas—its High Church, and its Low Church dogmas. And where is true Religion? where is the handmaid of our walking life, the blessèd beauty of the life of Nature? What contradiction is there in Spirit and in Nature? Does Spirit not inform, and vivify the pulse of Nature—does Nature not lend Grace its very outpour? True religion is the manifestation of all Grace; and Grace is not a *substitute*, but is a heavenly *graft* on Nature. Why was the heavenly God incarnate else?

Look at Nature—at its most beautiful and lovely thing, the spirit-feeling of the heart of Woman. What is the loveliest, holiest from God, the thing that is most beautiful in Woman—the typal thought that makes her being beautiful? It is the glowing up, and upward adoration. It is the sympathy of lovely feelings with all sterner life—the modest gait, the flood of generous heart, the verdant bloom of sweet affection on the lips. Is this the produce of theologic dogmas, of isolation and of talk? Dogmatic talk evaporates in talk—the rest is moral piety, and thirst for moral action.

Encourage in them thirst for moral action, and moral beauty will then grow—a daily sympathy with life, and *nature* will then grow. They are only spiritual, as they are natural—nature humanized by blessèd breathings, caught in daily work in the sweet air of Heaven. I love to see the tear of sensibility. It should be ever in the eye of Heart—a liquid drop, hazing, yet expanding vision, the too rigid vision. What a lofty, blessed truth is Charity.

Bright throeing of humanity, I love the genuine human heart. Its beat is the seraphic hymn of Earth—it marks the pulses of the world-great Universe. How mournful, alas! to be without it. There is a seed of beauty that is left, to dry upon the hour-glass sand, for each recorded second that we miss performance of a good work, filial of the God and human heart. Oh! what a world of wealth we miss, when one unwrought, good act, has passed us. A fruitful time, a season of our pilgrimage has missed; and we are barren of a treasured hoard, that joy and peace abounds from:—

" It is a blessed world—a theatre
  Where mighty purposes play out their parts :
  We see not half its beauty, till we *are*
  That which we see through love. The holy heart
  Fulfils the dream of olden alchymists,
  Turning all things it touches into gold."

There is a lovely spirit in Creation. It cannot be, that learned men will eat it out. And that is what they want, by their inventions in theology, to eat it out. What have the whole of them to say to vital spirit in religion? I am not going to except. I speak of all dogmatical extremists.

On one side, we are vexed with formalists—they are more than formalists, with tinkers and with formalists. The virgin allegorized with her flowing Cup—that other, with her Anchor—are not enough in their simplicity. The hood of a grave doctor now is on her. And then she flames in mystic garments, and a hundred candles without light are standing round her, and her glorious dual name is changed to—snuffers !

What is the little thing of human art that walks, and draws a circle round and round her, and writes upon the broad earth *orthodoxy?* And then, she lifts a wee small trumpet; and to the peoples of the Earth,. calls out—
' Come in, within my magic circle. It is illumined—
' bow to the true and blessed, the Apostolical succes-
' sion !' What rubbish is in learning. Oh ! for a cart, to cart it out, with the Apostolical succession.

But we are vexed with more than formalists—we have

the direr vexing of enthusiasts. Is here the simple virgin, with her cup and anchor of the soul? No, the
earth is not her beaten stand, to look with full cup on
the earth. It is not her beatific stand, uplooking meek,
to rest the anchor of her faith. There is an olden gib-
berish—a sort of lingual graft on the divine Apostles.
And all the earthiest common things have got ballooning
lights, and sail about in Heaven. Then all obscurest
mysteries—Almighty's high decrees, the ultimate pro-
phecies—are the familiar household word, expounded in
the fraction of its parts and last dread syllables. Up
goes the enchanted wand—and all the lowly beauty of
the earth, and all the moral beauty of the earth, and all
the beauty of utility, the spirit-walk of *act*, the great
regeneration's *living fact*,—are perishingly lost and
withered.

How does enthusiasm possess the soul? Is it all honest? or mingles there deception, and the self-decep-
tion? Oh! what a hideous fact, that the most earthy
and most sensual grow about the blessed things of Spirit and Religion. Oh! what a hideous fact, that, for
the pureness of the blessed things, we should throw out
Satanic imitation. We want to satisfy the carnal and
the earthy—we want a substitute for the heavenly
reality. Extremists are the natural growth of this dis-
tortion; and they fix upon, attach a mushroom growth
to non-essentials, whilst vitals starve, and, starving,
slumber.

Thus, the sobriety of life is sold; and knaves mix in

the gullible throng, and party-knaves swell out the tu-
mult, till the Christian body loses all the vigour of the
animated body, and starvelings roar a mimic drollery in
the land?

Is not extreme religion drollery? Mark—not the highest height of natural, and spirit-burst religion—but all
the mushroom growths of false religion, of devilry astride
upon the lowly back of pure religion. Dare such a thing
as this be constant tolerated in the land, while native
intellect, while genius and the power of intellect lives,
lives *useful* in the land?

Let intellect be useful in the land—let it set up the
pattern man, instead of aliening the shepherd's flock.
How many men now alien from the National Church,
who might be bulwark pillars of it. How many men
give countenance to separation upon non-essentials, who
shining hold and illustrate all true essentials. Gather,
gather round the National Church—bring all the wan-
dering strayers of the National Church into the heart
and body of the legal National Church. Organize the
power of the geniused intellect, and force enlargement of
the *basis* of the National Church.

Intellect is mighty, and can do it; but she must up
and stir, to do it. She must come about the pillars of
the venerated fanes, where Education hopeful nurtures
young desires in the people. Education grows with
young desires—true aspiring education. Then is the
season of organic fulness for the seed of breadth—thought
broadcast in the Nation. Oh! for a Church, the pillar

of the Nation. Oh! for a Nation, the pillar of the Church. When Church and Nation are symmetrical— moulding, intertwining, and identical. Glorious convocation—confederation of the Realm. This will be our high confederation—men and women of the Realm.

Men and women of the Realm—who, but themselves, are great as organs of opinion? This is a mighty theme—their *acts* are greatest organs of opinion. The moral acts of a Community are stronger than its laws. They are stronger than the strength of all its organization. In public Office, have I not shown it? The most efficient Heads, the most efficient Organization, will utterly fail, without the *moral* co-operation of the subordinate officers who have to work Departments. And what are all the functioned workshops of the busy breathing Realm, but the populated departments of the People's realm? I assert, that nothing throughout the great Community will prosper, without the moral co-operation of the working men.

And why? Moral is in league with all the confederated agencies which guard the ultimate pathways of success. They will not give the pass-word to bare enterprise. Bare enterprise breaks down, when Moral gives both thew and sinew to the work. Moral, only, can be *trusted.* That is its qualification and its power.

It is a mighty power; and, ramifying through all the acts of men, it is a mighty organ of opinion. When a Community is moral, morality allies with all its public aims — morality strengthens, and consolidates the issues of its naked enterprise. And thus, the separate and parted acts are never isolated. They are centered in the whole community, morality with the genius of its fine breath binding them. And thus, a time-got, practical elevation is produced—the elevation of a State, by the Heaven-guided elevation of its working men.

And shall we elevate its working men, and not most anxious cast a thought upon the elevation of its women? This is too neglected—the industrial advance, and elevation of its women. Is the Community not half made up of women—mothers of the Earth and women? What man ever thought like man, that did not think with tenderness upon a woman? All men are allied, at least to one that has the breast of Woman. What human man ne'er loved the breast that bore him? If there be a thing on Earth that does remind one of the abnegation of the souls of Heaven, it is a terrene mother. " You will think " me a fool," says Gray somewhere in a letter, "if I tell " you, that a man can have but *one* mother. A truism, in- " deed:—but one that no man ever knew, till he had lost " her, and for ever."

Many, many are the earthly mothers. Many join yet other bonds—bonds sweet and holy in the wedded sympathy. And there are many sympathies, all tender joining in the range of Woman's sympathies. Who has not known them, in devotion given?—always ready, balm and juice of freshest nature. What thing ever wanted —low or houseless, weak or friendless—if it had a crea-

ture want, that a woman was not there, to feed its want?
Weak—they are the pillar of the world's strength.
Beautiful—they are the last companions of its misery's
departing foulness.

> " The very first
> Of human life must spring from Woman's breast.
> Your first small words are taught you from her lips.
> Your first tears quenched by her ; and your last sighs
> Too often breathed out in a woman's hearing,
> When men have shrunk from the ignoble care
> Of watching the last hour of him who led them."

Does obligation make a debt, and how does Man repay
his sister Woman ?   Often, often, oh! too often, with
pollution.

Let me speak most plainly. How many of the noblest
sex are at this moment worse, miserably worse than if
they never had been born ?   Statistical details unfold a
state of facts, that is too shocking.   In the great City of
the Empire, 25,000 souls are prostitutes!*   And what

---

* I have given this, as the nearest approximation which I could
make, to a very moderate estimate of the number of prostitutes in
London.   There are no statistics, from the very nature of the in-
quiry, on which a perfect reliance can be placed; but the number is
variously stated, from the lowest Police return of about 8000, (which
is known, from the scope of it, to be far under the reality of truth,)
up to so high as 80,000.   Twenty-five thousand is stated to me, as
a reliable estimate, by the Secretary of one of the leading Metropolitan Institutions for the protection of Women, after having (he thus
writes) "placed himself, at the instance of Mr. Biggs, M.P., in com-
"munication with the Secretaries of all the Metropolitan Female
"Penitentiaries, and with many other gentleman who were known
"to have given attention to the subject, or whose official or profes-
"sional position was supposed to afford them the opportunities of

in all the Cities of the Realm? Thousands of the fair
sisters of the lords of this creation systematically made
brute of for their pleasure, and unspiritualized from the
likeness of true women. '
The very beasts, at least, are cared for. But these
wronged fellow-mortal women are not cared for by their
high abusers. Deprived of all that could make loving
feeling—deprived of all that could make peace and moral breathing—of the fruition of their youthful aspirations—of their homes and happy hopes—of that which
they inherited, their pure womanhood—they down de-
scend, the castaway of one, to be at last forlorn, and die
the death of vice in squalid rottenness.

Generosity and Man—ye are allied, when the foot
would crush the tender flower that looks up, and when
weak helpless life turns pitiful to be protected—ye
then protect. The guardian and unselfish foot stands
by, not *on* the helpless weak thing. And where is weakness, where is the tender flower that looks up—dewed

"judging." The Secretary to another leading similiar Institution
considered *double* that number to be not above the real mark,
speaking " after an experience of a quarter of a century."
Taking it at even this low estimate of my text, it is a shocking
thing to contemplate such wilful degradation of the noblest human
species. It is more shocking still to know, from the statistics of
these Institutions, how many (immensely large) are made so, at the
tender ages of from 12 to 17—almost without their mental degradation, but continued to their hopeless degradation, from the merest
absence of protection in their youth and opening servitude in life.
And these young creatures—who have never known almost what
virtue is—once they have entered on a course of vice, are found to
be the most hopelessly irreclaimable of the poor abandoned. The
deepest moral censure rests on those who deliberately, and habitu-

with feeling, the flower of the earth—your sister Woman? Is generosity not for your sister Woman?

Fairly think of them. Have they not interests—hopes buoyant with the blood of young life, just as men? They think, they over-think of life's alliance. It is most natural. The avenues of enterprise in the world are not ever open unto them. Over-leisure soon begets the unweeded crop of thoughts, desires, all the feelings that are still the brightest heritage, the blessing and the blight of women.

And must they ruthlessly be made the bane and blight of Woman? no antidote in Man—in fairness, sympathy, and the generosity of Man? Could every man not do a little, to be just, and fair, and sympathizing, and gene-

ally by their practice, *continue* to these outcasts the hope and the certainty of their unhallowed calling. They are the daily seducers of them, daily aliening them more far and far from virtue—instigating them to their earth's wreck, and pitilessly leading them to double death.

No power of the benevolent Institution can rectify this waste of soul and life. The daily food, for their compassion, will still be thrown to them :—but they can rescue, and do much to rescue. A vigilant supervision of the Metropolitan haunts of infamy—their emissaries and imps—and the assertion of the laws for the protection of women, they can dictate and promote. And they can seek out, and can shelter those who are in peril and unfallen, and shelter and reclaim the fallen ones. It is an eminent blessing, that there are such Institutions ; and they are worthy of every encouragement and support. I have received communications from the Secretaries of three of these in the great Metropolis alone ; and their Reports, transmitted to me, are worthy of the anxious perusal of the compassionate and benevolent. These are, " The Society for the rescue of " Young Women and Children," Office, No. 11, Poultry. " The " London Society for the protection of Young Females," Office, No. 28, New Broad-street. And "The Associate Institution for " improving and enforcing the Laws for the protection of Women," rous as Man? Ay, this little done by every man would do it all; and, without it, will be no part of that demanded recantation of the direst blot upon the fame and generosity of Man.

Laws, penal things, and legislature—what can they effect? God has stamped free will upon the world's condition; and that condition will be moral, when the gracious Giver of it shall permit the full appointed agencies in their maturity to work it. Woe to the man that is, of his free will, the potter's vessel of destruction. Woe to the man that sinks, of his deliberate will, the fellow-sister soul to her destruction.

Why should he sink his gentler fellow-sister to destruction? She may be of the common soul, unelevated

Office, No. 5, Upper Charles-street, Westminster. There are, in London, many of the regular Penitentiaries besides; and few of the large Towns in the Empire are without a similar organization, *to be supported.*

But there is an aim very much nobler, and more elevated far—that which is sought to be promoted in this Essay—to sap the root and the foundation of this evil in itself, and thus to lessen the neces-. sity for such Institutions in the world. This can be done, and only done, by the moral restraint of individual men. And the elevated and the good may all co-operate. Let them co-operate, to promote the industrial advance and elevation of the sex of Woman. Let them co-operate, to give a suitable employment to women. Let them co-operate, above all things needed, to give *remunerative* employment to women. And thus, they will co-operate to give the strongest stimulus to virtue in the sex of Woman:—that stimulus is, in God's superintending providence, by enabling them to obtain facility to independence first, and to legal union in the virtuous relations of Marriage. This is the aim, and the legitimate aim of every woman —in every rank and station of the world's society; and, in every rank and station where they are, it should be honestly furthered. There is the largest scope, where it is little practically thought of, in the middle classes of Society.

to know the depth of her destruction. This is a plea—
is it a generous plea? She may be of the common
soul:—but she can feel, and has her *better* feelings.
There was a time, when she had simple feelings—rude,
it may be, but associated with advance—her own advance, when some green sunny glade refreshed her, and
it was blighted. She was a Life, a living thing—who
offered her the poisoned chalice?

> " Yon insect on the wall,
> Which moves this way and that its hundred limbs,—
> Were it a toy of mere mechanic craft,
> It were an infinitely curious thing.
> But it has life, Ordonio! life, enjoyment!
> And, by the power of its miraculous will,
> Wields all the complex movements of its frame
> Unerringly to pleasurable ends.
> Saw I that insect on this goblet's brim,
> I would remove it with an anxious pity."

This pity, this beautiful outpour of pity for the crawl-
ing insect—none, is there to be none for Woman?
Who breathed a beautiful creation upon her, and left her
in the world, the helpmate of a guardian man? And is
not every man, by the solemnity of sacred trust, a guardian (where he finds her) of the feebler woman? Oh!
does the common Father ever look down on the violated
trust of Man? This trust is individual on Man; and all
the wrong, and foul corruption, must be wiped away by
individual man—how sure, how simple, and how glorious
telling—by individual man abstaining from the piteous
wrong to Woman.

But there are other agencies for the high and moral.
The root of evil must be sapped and taken; and stimulus must be given, and provision, to the industrial advance and elevation of the sex of Woman. It is vain to
hope for any melioration, while lavish idleness is left to
be the fosterer of vice. Expect not much of human nature, that is left to flood with its own baneful genders.
Vice genders in our nature, when there are absent all
the better, and the fruit-fulfilling things to gender.
And why should vice be suffered as the ill-conditioned
weed to gender, when there are flowers bearing precious
fruit to nurture?

Precious untilled, undeveloped grain and flowers—
women's fatherland—where is the land that fathers women? Is it Britain? They have, they have industrial
fathers in the Briton. But the fathers of their industry
must yet be many men, till they are father and paternal
of themselves, high race of women. Have they not
struggled nobly out? are they not struggling nobly out
in individual enterprise, named and famed in the wide
portals of the world? Have they not even left examples
of a purity in paths of Earth's pollution?—the Drama
and the Song, which they have made to be (associated
with them) worthy of their birth-descent from Heaven?

They are not only thus as high ambitious, and as independent. They are the beautiful dependent, helpmate of the strength and power of the world. I have a
feeling, that the softening and benignant influence of
women is but half applied, to temper and to meliorate

c

the world. When they shall mingle elevated, true utilitarian in the world, they will mould the ruggedness of the world. Let them mingle, let them mould and meliorate the world. Be this the mission of the men and women of the world.

Slow, very slow is all perfection. God omnipotent works it, and will work it. It is the end of all utility. Utility dawns on, dawns on—still growing from the creature work, perfection. And this will be—perfection. We see it now a budding, blossoming creation—we see it on and on, a newer blossoming creation. Thus, it will regenerate the world in time; and thus it will articulate its action:—the great mould of humanity shall soften, and the beams of the holy love shall brighten, and all be beautiful—the Sons of earth, and Daughters of the race, the parents of utility—and God will bless, and bring a blessedness about.

OFFICE, AND THE COMPETITIVE SYSTEM.

———◆———

I ADDRESS myself to working men, and to all working members of the public. It is their special interest—the subject of Competitive Systems and of Office. I have a claim, a double claim to speak, as having been a Literateur, and man of Office sometime in my passing day. I am not careful of offence—to high or low—I want to show my old companions up. I want to show how they are *vilified*, and how they justly *are* the vile. Mark me, I have nothing new—a few old facts put into their right place, and thus the public noddle straitened.

Long ago, mortality fell. It is an old hap; but as new now, in its day-brought effect, as if the fairest Eve was living. Somehow, we forget it always, and the poor Intellect is made to bear the burden of the protean incubus on Moral.

We hear of the incapables of Office; and we hear of the panacea, an *intellectual* competition, which is to give electric life to all that sit upon its wooden benches—to make its thousand elbows move as smooth as polished bone. What a thoughtful of—potato !

c 2

And is the crookedness of the serpent gone? Does Office here, to this fell root, owe nought, in its mighty mal-administration? Believe it, fallen brother—humble, *honest* work, is full of might; and, was it plied, would tell more than ten thousand *intellect* activities.

I do remember once a witty Judge, the incomparable Slick, describing our great office mansions, the mansions of the sleeping dead—" they looked, as if the tenants " were asleep." And so it is, if facts that do result are evidence of things. What is it, Office?—with its look, and its gait, and its somnolent grunt. I can liken it to nothing, but the attitude of a distorted hog, bristling with the incapable feathers of a goose!

But, brother, things are sometimes *more* than they do look. They sleep, but sleep a deeper sleep, than mere incapables of work. Go in, and live (as I have done) amongst them. I wish the witty Judge could spend a season, their familiar, in the sleep-look mansions. He'd find it out, of these same much misdeemed-of tenants —there was not a wink upon them.

Do as little as can be done upon a paper, is household office axiom. And then, to hear them curse and damn unhappy documents:—you'd think the writers were their enemies. The smallest workman pares, to make his small work smaller. Look at the humble registerer of a letter. The entry, that ought to be a careful abstract of the letter, is slovenly put; often, the most diligent searcher in the lapse of years, when it is vital to the pub-lic interests to trace it, can scarce discern that which he looks for, in the loose-recorded entry of it. Often again, though he may find it indexed to its place, the document itself is lost to practical access, by culpable neglect in noting local changes in the place of its deposit. And, when the public interests need it for a fact, the buried womb of paper-mass contains it.

. Take up, again, a lengthened correspondence. Read it from its outset to its end, and what is it?—the work of men, who never half-read the papers that they answered. Facts, dates, and things, are jumbled; beautiful confusion reigns; and sometimes the researcher asks himself at length—'fact, what is it'?

Indulge, my unofficial friend, a moment in the *theory* of approval, in a public Office, of an able Report. But let me tell you all about it. The writer diligently sifts, with carefullest research, the facts. He analyzes, and computes, and well applies his full experience and acquired learning, to meet the difficulty of dealing to assert a public right, or to supply a public want. He states the comprehensive view. He puts it full and clearly to the higher office, what the Public Service wants. And then he sits down, simple man, to think of the *effect* that must attend His document.

It is received, and duly registered. Junior Clerks have damned the writer as 'long-winded;' and $\frac{B}{24}$, received upon the Instant of the 1st, is duly put with papers to be acted on—next month! This is really a matter which cannot be disposed of in a hurry, and there is none, no hurry at all, about it. Taken up in the superior Office, it is at length; and the first proposition is, ' what's to be done upon it ?'

My unofficial friend, do you understand the meaning of 'a reference' ? Likely, you do not; and I will expound, as oft a doer of this act, the greatest acted of the public Office. Know then, it has *two* meanings—one, the abstract and ideal—the other, the practical and used.

The abstract thing means this. The Central Office, that is to judge, needs information from Professional, Art, or Local Sources, all existing in the organized officials of Department. The document, submitted to be judged, is sent to gather up the needful things which tell the Central Office how its recommendations would be like to work. And this is all most right. No man, or one man, could be a judge of how a recommended course may fit in with the many-membered sides of organizing which is wide-spread, detailed, complicated. And this is all most right. The perfect mind to judge, must be the *one* mind, and *instructed*. Instructed, it can read and judge with proper comments the original document. But does it read and judge, and are the proper comments to the document ? *There* is the practical—my unofficial friend—we touch upon the used and practical.

You must know, I should tell you here, that every man in a public Office is oppressed with public business! There is time, it is true, in the six hours of the working day, for healthful, spirit-giving relaxation—to play at pitch and toss, for jovial talk, to drink small beer. Oh! Mr. Justice Slick, if you could see at mid-day but the penetralia of a public Office, you would never, never say at spouting meetings, that its tenants were asleep. No matter—oppression reigns upon these innocents. And when 'a reference' comes, is it odd, or anything to marvel at, that the burden of the reference should be shifted ?

Office men, like other men, are imitative animals ; and they take a cue, as quick as any, from their masters. Lo, then, the document is opened ! And soon the diligent Clerk, who finds out nothing else, finds out—unspeakable grief for him to stomach—that the Central Office might have saved him half the trouble, by referring to their documents. Wisely thought, they knew that he had *copies* of them ; and then He thinks, as wisely thinks, if any subordinate office yet has other copies, or *copies of the copies.* Rejoiced to find it, the offending document is again enveloped, and duly goes down to the tail of office for report of fact. And thus, the Public's envelopes are spendthrift.

I would fatigue you, unofficial friend, to count up all the tortuous windings of this sample document. References, and sub-references, are on it—reports, and sub-reports, to answer. It goes about a-voyaging, till it finds at last the happy man who *guts* it !

Reader, if you are a lady or refined, pardon the expression. But there is nothing in all Johnson to convey the alchymizing, condensation-process, of ' bringing 'down' a public document, that dares to be efficient, to an understanding level to be acted on. Know then, the pith and bowels are taken out of it. Emasculated of its living value and its strength, the poor dead substitute—technical called Report—is forwarded. Well the cautious Clerk knows what his fellows at the Centre want; and, admirable man! he puts it all, (all *that* he puts,) to save the most oppressed of men the toil of reading this with any but a squint.

Poor innovator on the dead sea, Office—what a simple man you were, to waste your brains for nothing, but to have your head-piece thought eccentric. Myself, I recollect a high experienced one observing on the maniac act:—"I never do these things. I just get work approved. They will not read suggestive matter for "*their* act; but do not care, if work is broken up, how "many short things they pro formâ sanction." So it is, that office papers come to be the dry husks that they are—miserable lean—and everything that ought to be most searching looked, but covered by a generality.

There is amusement sometimes, of a mournful kind, connected with these office-paper orbits. I have told you of one of our high office axioms—the veritable thing, that public business very much its faithful officers oppresses. Another is, that these can do no wrong. Much I have considered it—something in myself, I boast, a little knowing in the Constitution. I draw it, then, from a participation of the Queen's prerogative. Are they not clothed (to borrow metaphor) in regal

petticoats, when, delegated, they administer the business of the Queen's own people?

The Heads of Office, they are lofty men. All central
acts, are acts of heads of office. And when the blunder-
ing mania takes, (for head implies not diligence or brains,)
then comes the delicate task on local and subordinate—
delicately to inform the official mind, that it has erred.

An answer to an unread letter (say) will come, as wide
astray from what was writ, as black from white—these
things, believe it unofficial, are quite common—and
then, you know, they can't *get* out of that. But, wary
mortal of subordinate clerk, He knows they must, must
be *let* out of it. The prudent thing is nicely penned,
directing the official mind to scan a certain part (the
very pith) that had escaped. And then an answer comes,
a dignified response:—' Sir,—Referring to your letter
' of the —— ultimo,' (to wit, the elder, and the cogi-
tated not,) ' and under the circumstances stated in your
' *explanatory* communication' (!)——I pass the rest.
The thing, you see, is done; and the poor Public, thus,
is often *done*. Admission is evaded, and the Centre is
infallible still.

It would be difficult, for any but the trained official,
to realize an adequate perception of the consistent *natu-
ralness* of Crimean or of Weedon happenings. They follow
—and a thousand similar which the Public never hears
of, only for the reason that they are an ever-growing,
but unblossom-happening—they follow from the cause
of the most utter apathy, and deadness to the moral sense

of duty, which pervade the salaried officials of the public Office. Sometimes, they have their root in mal-administration at the Centre; sometimes, at the Local Stations. But the Centre and the Local Station, all, are made up of the one dead mass—the morally untrained, and pulseless to a daily duty beating.

Not to speak of time, the valued time which is thus lost, it is not too much to say, that scarce a paper which originates is viewed in its full bearings, is dealt with as it ought. A loose and formal set of words is bandied round from each to each, that might apply to anything; and the real workman on a paper, no one finds in his legitimate place. Out-station men (the least remunerated) are made to bear the burden of all work. At Out-station, the paper really is *worked-up*. A spirit of a lazy heart is ever prompting at the Central Office to depute their work, till they become the mere recorders of what other men must work.

The very principle, the theoretic principle involved in 'reference,' is made the excuse; till it is wound about, a great red tape, to fetter energetic action, an incubus upon its pulsing heart. In my day, I have seen vast organic changes of Department. Before it, much the same took place. They mean all one thing—to carry out the over-centralizing, which puts place and patronage more thorough and complete at home. It has been the custom, true, to leave from time to time establishments enough, to counteract the disturbing evils of organic changes; but these have ever been the mere *transition* ones—establishments which had neither the power to apply their *own* abilities and energies to an efficient performance of the public duties, or to *resist* the hourly obstructing interferences caused by a want of local knowledge in the Central Office. They all, almost, in my day, now have passed away.

Theoretically, Centralization, as much as possible consistent with a true advance, is right. Uniformity in efficiency is attained; but there must be some provision, something far more than what now exists, to counteract the baneful evils of it from perversion, by the ministering officers, of its high intent. Uniformly, I have seen it end in one thing. The *administrative* duties which, under local Boards, were performed in responsibility by them, have been shifted over and transferred; and the performance, which was expected to issue from the Centre, never came. It was transferred back to the local Stations, in essence and substantially it was—transferred back to the mere *executive*, irresponsible for its administration—transferred too by a feint, a, tacit subterfuge, to countenance, under the forms of Office, dishonest and evading men to waive their duties.

The evils which result from detail ignorance, and from the conjoint effects of apathy and ignorance at the Central Office, are manifold. The interests, the most vital interests of individuals—those which concern their status and remuneration—are sacrificed; and a system of local toadying and jobbing is established, to recommend the rights which have not vent in the legitimate channels for their assertion. Every one is familiar with (for it is the household word of Office) the wrongs which a turn of the wheel of fortune will inflict. One man, after faithful service, will be cut down to a shilling; another, who has toadied through his life for final recommendation, will be liberally dealt with; another, who has earned position by his skill and honest front, is contumelious dealt with; while yet another, who has no living claim but *interest*, is propped up as the petted sheep, though numskull in an Office.

Acts, too, of the most hardened kind—acts for which a private man would soon be pilloried—are often, in the monetary public dealings, done. Few have lived much in the world, to whom these things, in some way or the other, have not come home. I speak but that which thousands know, and only put the explanation of it. It is to be explained by all that I have said upon the grade of moral of these men. The facts of any claim demand investigation and attention. That investigation and attention, rarely to them enough are given. Small are the sympathies of a man for his fellow-man, who is removed away at distance from him—whose moral action and whose work, appreciated often not because it is not understood, he does not witness. The natural sympathies of his kind, too, are biassed from him by self-interest:— for a saving of the public money is *commodity* to the man of Office, no matter how saved, by recommending him.

It is a strange thing—indeed it is not strange, when

thus considered, though it is anomaly—to witness zeal
from those who are not zealous. But it is an undeniable
fact, that the very same men who in office are most lax,
most reckless of the public papers that they act on,—if
a money-claim, or anything to check a money-claim, is
submitted,—they start into galvanic action, as if their
moral intellects were quickened. Oh, my public pocket!
Round about the paper goes; and, if the claim can be
ignored, or any flaw by red tape seen—the *moral* claim,
no matter—the man of zeal is up; he makes the member of the public know, that law is on its legs!

Gentle unofficial, do not think that I am telling you
that Jobs are at an end. No—but every man is not the
man, that's worthy of a job. Jobs, I would have you
well to know, are jobbed as much as ever; but, in the
office of the Public, *discretion* must be used. It is a
jewel, as said of old, and charity begins—at home!

This Central Home—by all accounts, it is a comfort-
ablehouse; but comfort is not the heritage of scullions,
and they must put up with their better's leavings. Why,
then, should lodgers on the great domain expect the pay
of servants in the upper house?—these men are long-
headed. Bless their long heads, strange thoughts will
sometimes be the tenants.

Reader, have you ever laughed, to see an Ass's head
enveloped in the dignity of cravat? Behold it, when
the womb of Office mighty throes; and some con-
figuration on the head of Organizing is wafted, in the

stately language that the semi-demi-Gods invent. Pre-
monitory warnings—'shadows,' in the Poet's language,
'of the great unseen'—come first before to tell it. Then,
the mighty womb delivers; and, lo, there comes out
——a Rat!

How often have I seen it hunted. Something crude,
unfitted to amalgamate with what existed—something
that neither could be made to work, or would let other,
that was working, work—the product of a silken man
that sat on carpets, to crow tunes for music at the Stations—a master-mind, that took its cues from theoretic
fancies; and wouldn't do, till he made *bodies* fit the
jackets that he cut.

All things find a level, and, in the public Office, soon
they find their level. Men are not adapting monkeys
always, and the public business finds its proper channels; but the big man must be humoured. A formal
and apparent thing is done, obedient to the mandate.
Another form is formed, the tape-roll more unwound,
to clog the wheels of Office. For all, they know the
Rat is hunted. The little vermin will not *work;* and it
must hide, as soon as it hides, a skulker in the dusty
paper.

Cravat for the Ass!—how many of the world, and of
the big ones of the world, weave but cravat for the Ass!
Portentous seeming, big-word utterance, smoothness,
and potato-polish—how the world licks it up! It is
most juvenile; and so impostors thrive, and eat it out of

heart. But I must talk of Office, and of its rare impostors yet. Indulge with me, my unofficial friend, while I unfold the very cranium of it broken.

You are a man, with flaws in your morality; and do not think, because you are not seated upon desks, you are a whit the better. It is not Office-man, but Man, that fails *in office.* This is the pith of all my argument; and every calling will exhibit contraries between its office-actings and its folk. Look at the Military man, as I have seen, when he has sheathed his sword, and taken up the harmful weapon of the pen. He is an amiable man, and very good, right honest, liberal with his fellows. Put him to it, and he will drink fire on a bomb-shell! I love these men, sometimes, when I do read about them. Honour, honour to their valour and denying acts—honour to their kindliness when warring strife has ceased, and brotherhood is welcomed to cheer on the social life.

But put the man, the very man, to govern in an Office ; and strait he carries all his littlest prejudices with him. He carries his contempt of all Civilians, his under-formed notions of their skill in their vocations, his crudest thoughts about their workings and vocations. The official Clerks, (who are it may be by their birth, as much as he is, gentlemen,) he comes to look upon as verily no better than his bombardiers, born for his elevated service. He coolly takes the product of their skill and brains, appropriates it, signs it as his own; and this would all be well if he appreciated, and could learn enough to tell their masters, and his masters, what the underworkmen worked.

But how can Law, how can Divinity know physic? And how can man of War know law, divinity, or physic? No more can he know of the tithe of things, the crafts, vocations, that are exercised, to supply the detail vast‑ness which is ministered for in the public Office. And yet, in spite of this, and of the evils which it works, the Military Offices are crowded with the sword and cocked-hat, thrust into the very needle and the distaff.

At humble distance, I have seen Lords and Peers of Realm; but I never *felt* my distance, or my utter dis‑tance, but when I beheld a Colonel of the drum, with cracked-brain pen a-drumming. You'd think the man, as Poets say, was "forming," or "creative forming." There he sits, lord of the best office, in his costume. A pile of papers lie, which, if he told the truth, are Arabic to him. No matter—he can sign them. He can put into his military pocket the reward of sweat of brow of the Civilian. He can snub him. He can arrogate to his most little self the merit of the toil, the brains, the sweat of brow, the efficient working of the Office which, of his own brains, he could not carry on a week.

It is commendable to distinguish, and to reward the bravery of the brave, to elevate them where their proper talents to the Country may be useful; but it is a gross perversion of the public patronage, to promote them into place and office where they are most alien, legitimately where they have no function, and where the Military presence is an incubus upon the rise and just reward of Civil merit.

A very kindred evil unto this, next calls for observation—the status, in the public Office, of the professional. I believe that to every, at least to most of them, a public Solicitor is attached. Few Departments of the Public have not property, or dealings, many ways, in legal monetary things and property. The presence of a man of Law becomes, for daily current use, a necessary. And in a large Department, and with a large extended property, it would be difficult to realize (if one had never witnessed it) the magnitude and the monetary importance, the intricate difficulty of the questions, that are hourly depending on his skill and judgment for decision. The Law Officers of the Crown are made auxiliary; but the cases where they are consulted are comparatively few, and, in the aggregate, form an inconsiderable portion of the legal professional business done by the Departmental Solicitor.

I am restrained, for reasons of a private duty, from adequately entering on this topic. It would demand a statement of the special facts, which would be out of place, unfitted for the Public. Let it be enough for me to speak, in greatest brevity, of how the character and the qualification of the persons work, affecting the administration of the public business.

I have no hesitation in saying, as the result of all my observation on it, that the position of a Departmental Solicitor, controlled by unprofessional men, is not defined enough to insure its efficiency. If he is efficient, (and I very much doubt if a mere Solicitor is generally in the legal attainment adequate,) his efficiency is marred too often both by ignorance on the part of his controllers, and by interference. If he is not efficient, both control and proper interference are precluded by ignorance. I have seen the public Board in both predicament. I have seen them helplessly incapable of exercising the powers which they had, to force on any right performance of the duties on the legal references, foiled in every effort by an ignorance of knowing what the legal officer could and ought to have done. I have seen them exercising the powers which they had, upon the other hand, to thwart and hamper all efficiency.

It is not possible, but when the thing is by professional observation witnessed, to realize the utter folly of the acts which hamper legal officers; and not so much the hampering acts, as acts (behind them done) that hamper. There is almost an utter ignorance of *where*, and *when*, the right occasion; and duties are thrust upon unprofessional officers, (and this is daily in Departments growing,) which these officers have no faculties of the kind to perform. No capability, even where it does exist, can confer the *acquired* capacity to deal with that which demands the application of a professional learning; and the public interests, which are trifled thus, are of the gravest magnitude, in the imperilling of territorial rights, and in the wasteful gendering of responsibility. Until the public property of Departments, and the arrangements for its daily dispensation, shall be brought within the control and the direction of a responsible and qualified Department of Public Justice, nothing but weakness and disorganization, and public losses can result.

Have I then said enough, in this rapid cursory of a few of the most prominent evils resulting from the moral grade of public Officers, to vindicate the affirmation at my opening,—that there is more besides the qualified education of the Intellect demanded, to make candidates for Office fitting. Far be it from me to lay it down, that honourable exceptions are not found amongst the ranks of Office, who redeem it from a universal moral dereliction. I know it that there are, and that there ever are such. Life's universal walks exhibit it, and why should Office not? The business of the public Office is too demanding, to be all reckless done; and these few men—they are an honourable few— support the burden of it on them.

Look into any public Office, if you can look upon its inmates and its work; and tell me, are its workfolk _all_ its working men? No—the mass are copiers and extractors, unfitted to be else. There is no equal distribution of the business, that is real. The head-work is the work of one or two who over-work, to make up for the absent vacuum of the rest. Honour to these honourable men. The world little knows them; but I have known them, and I make my humble tribute that I honour them.

They are not merely the Civilian—they are not mere the Military man. Both have the excellent official, and soon they are found out. Work has a true instinct; it always finds the workman, and the able workman gene-. rally is willing. Soon they are found out—found out by those who want to use them, but never, in the public Office, by the ones who ought to honour and promote them.

Are these things right? and is it right to tolerate a public degradation,—that the men of might, in every world's calling, should be eminent; and only, in the high administration of the Country's business, that they should be nameless skulking? Is it right that affluent means, the public Salaries, should be held and eaten out by oysters?—sucking creatures on a bed, that open up their shells, and gather comfort. Are not the tenants of the public Office incubating? Are they not doing anything, but *working*? And, then, the working Public must do work, to pay the jobbing item of the taxing.

There is a cause—there is a remedy, in looking to the cause, for these things. The cause is want of moral intellect, and not the mere lack of the intellect. It is an error to suppose, that there is absent organization. There is always measure of it quite enough, if there was application in the workmen. The business of the world is not so difficult, but that the humble faculty may work. God has so ordained, that much the larger mass of Mankind are the lowly workfolk, small, but busy in Earth's territory. Humble, *honest* work, is full of might; and, was it plied, would tell more than ten thousand *intellect* activities.

Again, I here assert it. Fearless I assert, that intellectual competition never will give men, fit men for Office places. There must be intellectual, moral *training*. There must be organized a system *educational* for such training. Examination may turn up a clever one —perhaps, too clever for his station. He may be only a crammed specimen. The very faculty to show a cram, is that the least auspicious for the making of the sober workman.

What are the qualities required in the office workman? Let me tell you. I am not biassed. I have been a literary, and an office workman.

The office workman must know how to Read—not print, but the most illegible of what his brother workmen write. He must know how to Write:—unless he is a Head of Office, he must know how to write. Mark it:—Heads of Office *spider*, they do not *write*. He must be qualified in Number, and know the art to tot. He must have local Geography, and tell how travellers go. And then he must have Composition for his office-brother's thinking, and after for his own. He must have general Intelligence, and this the chiefest head-thing. Above them all, he must have Diligence, and evidence of moral Heart. He must have promise of a Christian earnestness, the sum and summit of it all. If he has these, he has what makes the right man in an Office, the fit man in his place. He has the *elements ;* and, doubt not, that the fulness of his stature all will grow.

Can the searching of a one examination show out such a man? Can answers of the stuffed head tell the answering of the trained thought and the heart? Acquirement is no acquirement, unless it moulds the individual; and can a passing question, can any passing searching, tell the high mould of the individual? Believe it not. The power of lengthened observation must concur—the power of lengthened culture after, in the working office, must produce him.

The thing, so far, that we have shown, is then the *academical* desideratum, to educe and to result a proper basis of election. The acquirements of literature, the acquirements of craft, may then be got, the training and the discipline. Qualified judgment can select them— the trained, the disciplined, the competent of craft— then only can select them.

Do we raise a rival to the organized academies of University? No—we would *apply* them. Are they for professional, and is not Office a profession? Though it is left a howling waste, it is a noblest of professions. Every calling is in its compass. The world's variety of wants, the Public want, no less than members of the Public; and Office is a thing the most wide, and adapting. Its rudimental acquirements are only the acquirements for doing at a young beginning, though grayheads show (disgrace to Office constitution) the rudimental elements for ever only of beginning.

There is a poverty of expression, a mind expanded by
no liberal education, intellect unused, a stereotyped letter for *all* uses. There is a want of aptitude for special
application, an absence of impulsive energy, and of the
disposition for research which education gives. There
is a baldness on the juvenile, a head unclothed upon—
all things in privation, which the academies of life give
to the young man, *education*. And this is not an acquisition, but a moulding. It does not serve a purpose,
but when moulding. Its specialties, its facts, its all
indoctrinating, are to mould him. And does it mould
him? That is the true test, the test of right in the successful competition.

·And does the educational acquisition mould him?
It is the question that must be asked, to answer if the
successful candidate of trial will endure the working
trial, as an office workman. It is the question still that
must be asked, to answer it at every stage of upward
progress in the working office. It *inspirits* him. He is
the working workman only, if the educational element
inspirits him. 'Does it inspirit him?'—will a competitive examination to this question answer?

It will not answer; but intelligent observation, of sufficient length, will answer—intelligent results, throughout sufficient length, will answer. More yet, the same
will answer. The qualification of the *moral* fitness, they
will answer—does the moral, with the educational, inspirit him? Thus, there is the Academical desideratum.

Competitive examination is a glorious thing. Organized with a system educational for office training, it will meliorate the working Constitution. It rebukes a foul abomination; as it is an inroad on the jobbing, and the place-hunting policy of the past. What has been the policy of the past?

The prominence of political parties—it has been the policy of the past. The prostitution of the public patronage, to subserve political parties—it has been the policy of the past. Thanks to the great Dispenser ordering providence, the world has begun to see to *all* political parties, and the hollowness of their creeds. There is nothing, which the course of times has made so manifest as this,—that the distinctive differences of parties now are vanishing, and are leaving, for the partisan, nothing to declaim on but the *personal.*

What speaks the Parliamentary Session—Session after Session—I ask, what speaks the Parliamentary Session? It speaks of lowness and of parties. It speaks of one uprising, and another falling—the business of intrigues and combination. It speaks of orator's froth, and of debating. It does not speak a word of vital framing, to meliorate the Constitution. Parliament sits to vote expense, and to depute political rogues to fill up places. What a hot-bed of a rotten frame we live in?

And this is all for *places.* Respectable John Bull, *you* must unbutton, to qualify political rogues to fill up places. What a cuckold they are making of you! The places are your own domain, and, of your promise-sons,

the born inheritance. Will *you* feed bastards with your
riches? Are they not bastards?—when false Governors
prefer, to places of the competent, their pigmiest creatures—are these the Sons of England, or its bastards?

There is a glorious Constitution rising. I see it in
the changing shapes of world's political fashion. I see
it in the Public's growing voluntaryism, and in the public great distrust of Senate and its laws. British man
will govern himself. I see it in his high determination.
I see it in his growing aptitudes, and in his myriad-grow-
ing impulses and energies. I see it in his high adven-
ture—*his* soul-enterprise, a thousand ways intelligent
directed. I see it in its noblest manifest—the freed
spirit of his emulation.

And shall he not be left to emulation? Shall men,
politically governing, be tolerated to rob him of the
fruits he might aspire to, as the noblest subject for his
emulation? Shall they, for British candidates, pawn
calf-heads on the Nation? Away with them—take
public patronage from them—British man will govern
himself.

I see a glorious Constitution rising. Office, with the
skilled and true, will yet be filling. It must with them
be filling, till the Office of the State is opened as *profession*. And when the Office of the State is opened as
profession, it will result in noblest fructifying. Invigorating the State, it will educe the elements of Statesmen. Every intellect, that now is aliened, will flow in-
stinctive plenteous to it; and, chiefest, Literary enter-

E

prise, will yet be more than what it is—the heritage of beggars.

Onward, Britain! Take public patronage from Statesmen, and you will find the way to make them Statesmen. Yourselves will be your Statesmen—in the Office of the State, you will be working men and Statesmen. Onward, onward, Britain!

NOTE.—It is, perhaps, right to anticipate here an objection which may be made to the practicability of any movement, having for its aim and object the melioration of the public service, to arise from the introduction of the Academical element into the system of competitions for public Office, with a view, especially, to obtain a practical attention to the desideratum and necessity of looking to the *moral*, as well as to the *intellectual* qualifications of the candidates.

My eminent friend Professor Fairbairn, in a recent letter upon this subject to me, very judiciously and ably remarks, that "the " great difficulty, perhaps, would be, to constitute any test by which " it should be tried, or to apply a test, so as to secure impartiality " and public confidence. I am afraid, (he continues,) that, before " any satisfactory system could be devised for these ends, the public " would need to make considerable advances in the path of high " principle and Christian worth. The vital sap will have to rise " from below, and diffuse its invigorating influence through the " trunk and branches, before much can be done with the glittering " blossoms at the top. Let us each do what we can in our respec- " tive spheres, and with the talents God has committed to us, and " we shall at least contribute something towards the desired result. " Only a morally healthful Community can bring a wise and proper " distribution of public trusts—to the extent that it should be done " —in a professedly Christian Country."

To these remarks, coming from so profound and elevated a thinker as Professor Fairbairn, I have directed a marked attention, in framing the observations (page 26) which constitute the last division of the topics of the preceding Essay,—the necessity of which was indeed suggested to me thus, as well as by my eminent countryman Mr. Napier, commending the suggestions of Professor Fairbairn. But, so far as they have a special reference to *this* Essay, I would only say, (as I have said to him in explanation of the scope and purport of it,) that my aim was more to draw attention to the great fact—which is fundamental—of the *moral* desideratum for Office, than any way to work its application or details. I have ever found, in my experience, that it is in vain to present a *total* view to men. When the public mind is very much opposed to entertain a disagreeable aspect of the heavenly truth, we miss all, if we try too much, and men are very much satisfied with the measure of their own morality. They must first apprehend the *generality* of the moral desideratum for Office, and then you may chance to get a field for *more* intelligence.

Upon the whole, I am very much disposed to consider the tests of preliminary entrance upon Office, as only a small part of a system of true competition—competition that will throw up true men for the current service of the public. There must be larger agencies applied, and there must be more continuous agencies. Little can be done, till the Academical Institutions are more powerful in the Country—till the Literary genius and its enterprise are practical and more powerful, moulding the Academical Institutions of the Country.

It is, therefore, to the topics of overflowing interest, in the Essay on Society, that I look for the true solution of our National difficulty—not referring to the difficulty of official administration solely—but to that which is involved in the grander-interesting question, of the general interests of the Country. No one, candidly viewing the arguments of that Essay, could doubt that there are vast agencies for good, in the political arena, which are slumbering, and which would give (if rightly moved) a different aspect to things. Indeed, the state of our Constitution is most perilous ; and peremptorily calls on all good men to co-operate, for the application of better public agencies.

There has been, for years past, a gradual yielding to brute power —uneducated, unqualified, and much every way unfit to use it. Such a state of things must gradually tend to anarchy, and to prepare the way for a Military despotism, that will crush our true liberties. Power never yet was given to those unfit to use it, but they *abused* it, by handing over to the first adventurer. And yet, the People are not incapable of being worked and led. They *are* led, and always led by knaves, when honest men hold back from leading them. Every intellected man in the Community should be up *utilitarian*—it is imperative on them—or the British Constitution will be lost. The vast pernicious Centralizations, which have been for years past taking place in the Executive, are preparing a state of things, that, coupled and along with the gradual extinction of the proper powers of the Legislative bodies, will yet be instrumental (if not beneficently averted) to hand over all power to the Military delegates of the rabble.

It behoves the British people, to be up and stirring. The Revolution is but slowly culminating ; and the people see obscurely, how the progress of events is tending. They have aversions, where they ought to have no feeling of aversion, to conservative upholders of the Constitution. And they have misguided preferences, that are leading them to give a preference, unmistakeably, to political abortions.

Conservative leaders must be liberal, and comprehensive in their ken. They must enfranchise Property, and Intellect, and Enterprise. It is plain, to every thinking man, that the proper principle of enfranchisement, adapted to the present aspect of the Constitution, is to enfranchise at a *low* property qualification. It must be done, because the palpable fact is, that there is power *there*. But it is equally demanded, too, to counteract, by all proper means, a pernicious working of it. That must be done, by the largest measure of enfranchisement—ay, and *double* enfranchisement, wherever it can be practically introduced—of the skilled and educated, and of the *intuitively* skilled and educated by the gift of natural enterprise.

The glory of this Country is, its aristocracy—its making, made, and to be yet made aristocracy. They are the symbols, in the Country, that the *eminent* have rank—that we transmit it, with the lustre of hereditary rank. The eminent must be—not circumscripted, as the eminent, by the heritage of land—but all the eminent. The Commerce of this Country, its industrial Art, is a possession as solid as its land. It is more spiritually allied—it is outstretching—bearing to the distant land the power, and making distant land the wealth of Britain. Its Cities and its Towns are fruitful, as the producers and emporium of it. They are not severed from the Counties—they stand, as luminous, and opulent of greatness, *in* the Counties.

I will not enter on the special questions of the Franchise. They are important ; but, compared with others that I have dwelt on in the Essays, they are of little moment. The able and the eminent man will always have *his* influencing place, and always influence *in* his place. The Public, as a mass, are always led. Our highest duty is, to see that they have leaders—*leaders*, not *political intriguers*,

THE END,